For Isla and Charlie — L.S.

This story was inspired by my sister Maisie's real life
dog Ralph, who one day, met some ducklings...

First published in 2021 by Scholastic Children's Books
Euston House, 24 Eversholt Street, London NW1 1DB
a division of Scholastic Ltd

www.scholastic.co.uk
London • New York • Toronto • Sydney • Auckland • Mexico City
New Delhi • Hong Kong

Text and illustrations copyright © 2021 Lorna Scobie

HB ISBN 978 0702 30401 9
PB ISBN 978 1407 19250 5

Printed in China

10 9 8 7 6 5 4 3 2 1

The moral rights of Lorna Scobie have been asserted.

Papers used by Scholastic Children's Books are made from wood
grown in sustainable forests.

LORNA SCOBIE

DUCK, DUCK, DAD?

Ralph enjoyed a quiet life.
He liked going on quiet walks to smell
the flowers, past the butterflies and trees,
past...

...an egg?

CRACK!

Ralph wasn't sure that he wanted a duckling.

But the duckling wanted him.

Dad?

It didn't seem very quiet.

But, at least it was just the one.

Ralph wasn't at all sure how to look after his new ducklings.

They **definitely** weren't quiet.

But he decided to have a **go**.

They needed things **all** the time.

Did ducklings eat...
Dog food?
Broccoli?

Ralph wasn't sure sweets were quite the right food for ducklings.

MORE PLEASE!

But they seemed to like them.

Bath time was even rather fun...

...most of the time.

Sorry, guys!

And Ralph got bedtime cuddles just right.

Another story?

Night, Dad!

Sometimes it was lovely and quiet...

...but just for a while.

Ralph was almost beginning to enjoy his new noisy life.

Things were going very well...

Are we nearly there yet?

UNTIL...

OH! Thank goodness I've found you!

Life with his new family certainly WASN'T QUIET...

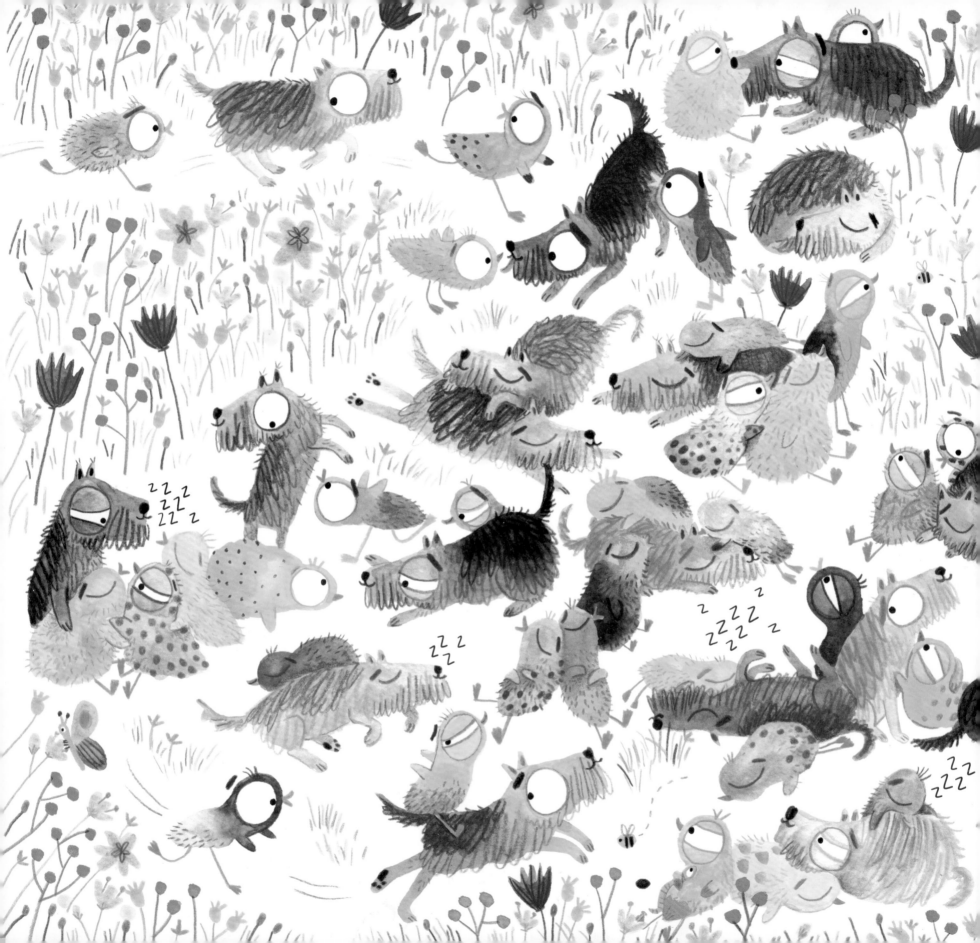

But it was full of CUDDLES!

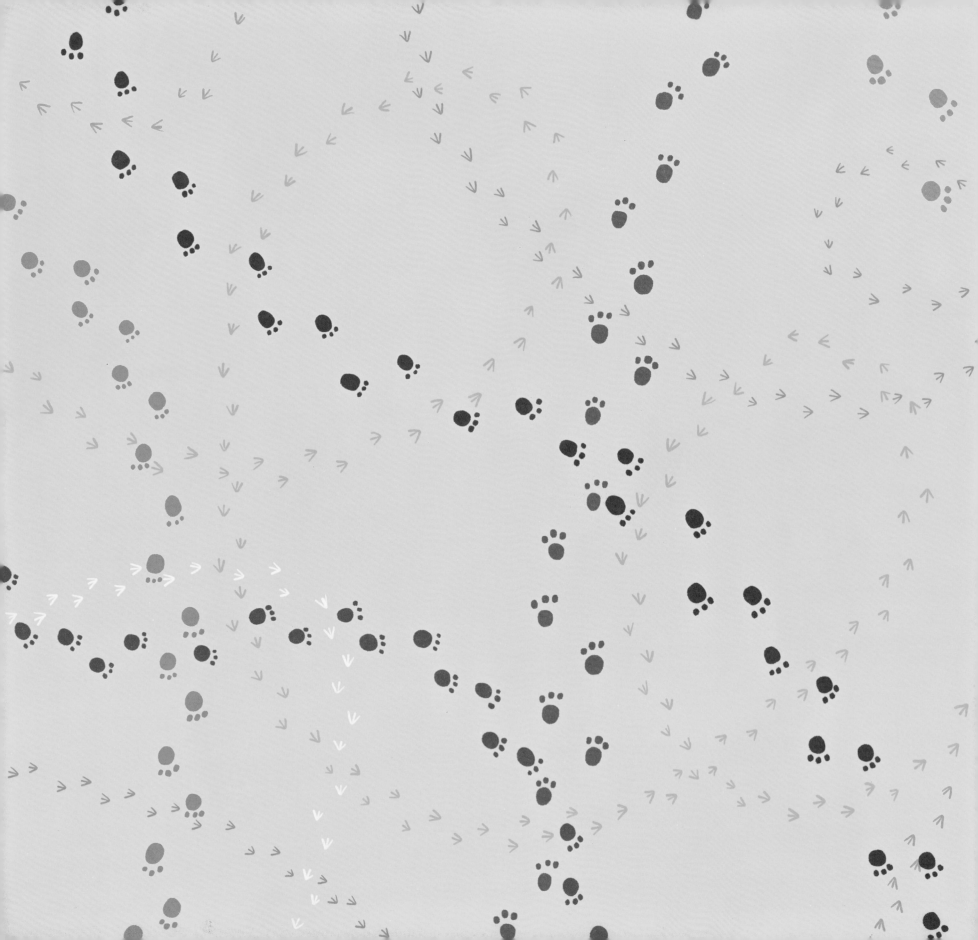